For our sweet Cassius.
Always remember to try, try again!
Love - Mom & Dad

D0521001

As the sun slowly woke and rose up high,
she brightened and warmed the blue summer sky.

"Little Bear," Mama said, "today is the day! Your first game is here! Are you ready to play?"

Eagle, Bear, Beaver, and Moose –
the team was about to be set loose.

Lacrosse was the game that brought them together,
and the start of a friendship they'd remember forever.

They huddled together, stood tall and steady.
They had practiced hard and knew they were ready.

They walked on the field and got into position,
each player determined to conquer a mission.

The big game had started
and faceoffs were fast!
Beaver was mad
he kept coming in last.

"Get low to the ground,
lean in and clamp.
Time the whistle
and you'll be the champ!"

Moose was on defense protecting the goal.
He almost stopped Rabbit, but saw a wee mole!

The wee mole came out running right under his feet,
and sadly resulted in Moose getting beat.

Coach Owl talked to Moose.
"When you're angry don't holler!
Remember your size,
stand up and play taller!"

Dodging and shooting, Eagle showed off his skill,
but stumbled one time and took a bad spill.

"It's OK, Eagle, don't stop trying!
Keep your head up and soon you'll be flying!"

Bear stood in goal making saves with his stick,
but sometimes the shots came in way too quick.

Coach said, "Listen Bear, pretend you're a wall. You must be brave and attack the ball!"

Players ran to the huddle.
The first half had finished.
It was clear to the stands
that the team felt diminished.

Coach said, "Keep on trying and rise to the test.
Trust in yourself and play your best!"

The players were tired - sweat down to their laces.
Despite this exhaustion, they all took their places.

The second half started and Beaver stayed low.
He won all the faceoffs and stole the show!

Moose was determined to use his large size.
His plays were smart and his defense was wise.

Bear used his courage and stood like a wall.
He felt very brave and made all the balls fall!

Eagle remembered to keep his head high.
He saw the field well and started to fly!

The score was so close,
but the game was now done.
It had been a long struggle.
Coach Owl's team had won!

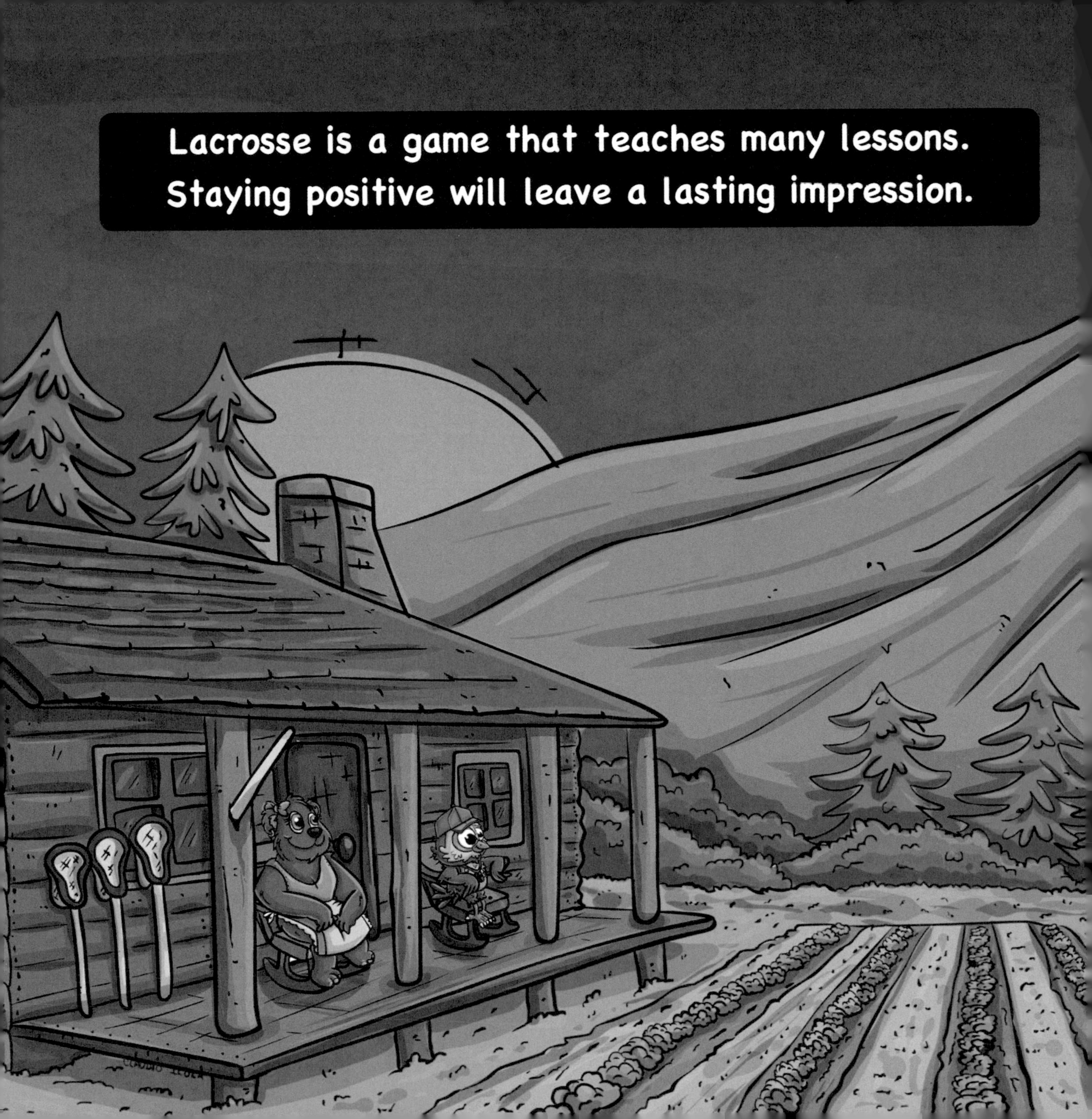
Lacrosse is a game that teaches many lessons.
Staying positive will leave a lasting impression.